Pony Express
to the Rescue

by Cameron Cook
illustrated by Bob Dellinger

Harcourt

Orlando   Boston   Dallas   Chicago   San Diego

Visit *The Learning Site!*

www.harcourtschool.com

Like many other farmers and ranchers, the Bede family had come to town to watch a special event. Soon they saw a cloud of dust and heard hoofbeats. Then the Pony Express rider dashed into town! Everyone cheered. The mail he was carrying had come to California all the way from St. Joseph, Missouri. It had not taken months, as it always had before. It had taken only a little more than a week!

"It's the start of a new time," Mr. Bede said to his wife, Cora, and their daughter Martha. Then they rode back to their ranch.

The Bede family raised cows. Their ranch did not make a huge profit. Even so, Mr. Bede often said he would rather be a rancher than do any other job.

"Tell me more about the Pony Express," Martha said to her father when they got home. She was his oldest daughter. They were out in the fields, tending the herd. Together they were looking for stray cows to put back in the corral. From there, the cows would go to market.

"The Pony Express hires young men," Mr. Bede said. "They must be strong and ride a horse very well. Most importantly, they must be brave. The trail across the country is not always easy. They never know what the weather will be like. These riders must be very light, too. That way, the horse can run quickly when carrying both the mail and the rider."

"The riders change horses every 15 miles. Then, after about 75 miles, a new rider takes over. To think that mail can travel so far so quickly! The Pony Express comes all the way from Missouri here to Sacramento, California.

"It costs a lot of money to send a letter by Pony Express. But if you ever need to send something quickly, this will be the best way to do it."

The next day, Mr. Bede called to his wife. "Cora? Have you seen my medicine?"

Mrs. Bede came in. "No, Charles. Did you look in our medicine chest?" she asked.

"It's not in there!" Mr. Bede said. He sounded scared. They looked everywhere, but the medicine was missing. Martha knew that meant trouble. Her father had a serious health condition. If he didn't take his medicine, he would become very sick.

"What will I do?" Mr. Bede cried. He put his head in his hands.

Then Martha spoke up. "What about the Pony Express, Papa?" she asked. Her father looked up.

"That might work," he said with a nod. A Pony Express rider was due in the next day. He could send a message with him. The medicine could return on the next trip. "It will cost a lot of money," Mr. Bede said.

"Oh, Charles, don't even think of that!" Mrs. Bede said. She set out to town to give the message to the Pony Express.

The next day, the Pony Express rider arrived at the station. "There is a very important letter in there," the postmaster told him. "A rancher needs his medicine. Take care!"

The rider was off, heading east toward Missouri. Many days of rain had turned the trails into mud. In the first 20 miles, the rider changed horses three times!

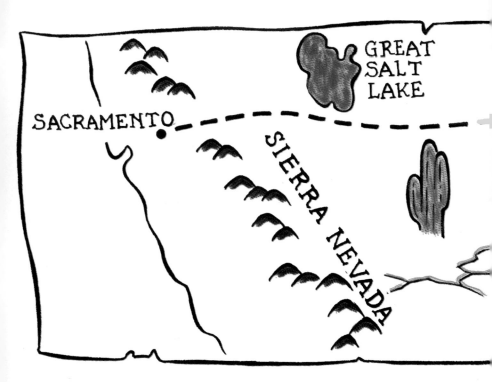

Soon the trail got even worse. It was steep and slippery. Rain kept falling. The horse slipped several times.

Then the rain turned to sleet. The next time the horse slipped, it fell. The rider was thrown to the ground. However, he got up and made it to the next station. There he got a fresh horse.

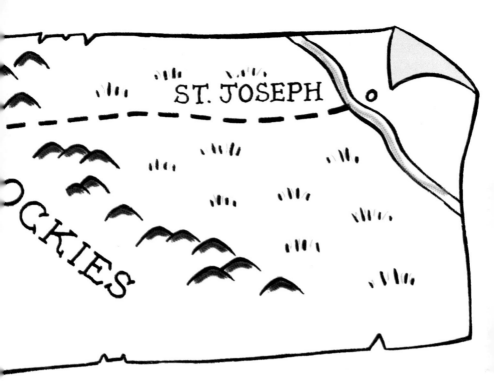

The rider covered 60 miles in the rain
and sleet before another rider took over.
As that rider crossed the Sierra Nevada
Mountains, he had to make his way
through huge snowdrifts. The route was
steep. Slowly, the horse and rider inched
ahead against the harsh wind.

The third rider had to ride through the
desert. The weather was hot, and he was
thirsty. The horse kicked up sand as it ran
east toward Missouri.

The rider waved his hat as he sped past a
wagon train. The people on the wagon train
looked on in wonder. Who was that rider?
He seemed to have come from nowhere!

The last rider ended the trip in St. Joseph, Missouri. A doctor there got the letter that day. Quickly, he counted out pills for Mr. Bede and put them in a box. He gave the box to the Pony Express rider who was heading back west. "Take care!" the doctor told him. "That medicine may save a rancher's life!"

"You bet, Doctor," the rider said as he tipped his hat.

Back at the Bede ranch, the family waited. Mr. Bede was feeling sicker and sicker. He stayed in bed. But the work of the ranch had to go on just the same.

Animals still had to be fed. Stray cows still had to be put in the corral. Martha and her sisters spent their time tending the herd. It was hard to work when they were so worried about their father. When would the Pony Express come?

The Pony Express riders were heading
west toward California as fast as they
could. The first one handed off the mailbag
to the next with the medicine safe inside.
That rider raced across the windy
Nebraska prairie. The third rider carried the
mail through a snowstorm. The next rider
rode through sleet in Utah.

After a week, the Bedes got word that
the medicine was in town. The Pony
Express had come through!

Mrs. Bede raced to town and came back with the precious box of medicine. She raised her husband's head and gave him a tablet.

In a few days, Mr. Bede was feeling better. Forever after, he would tell the story of what happened. "Yes, indeed!" he would say to all the ranchers. "I owe my life to the Pony Express."